# The Women Who Settle

### ZOI VICTORIA

# DEDICATION

This book is dedicated to all the girlies in the world.
You is smart.
You is important.
You is special.
Your Life Matters.

# CONTENTS

1   The Pleaser   3

2   The Prodigy   13

3   The Enabler   21

4   The Hurt Healer   31

5   The Drunk   41

6   The Mother   51

*Acknowledgements and Love* 57

# The Women Who Settle

THE WOMEN WHO SETTLE

# 1 THE PLEASER

"He took everything out of the accounts. Our bank account, our savings account, everything is just gone." Charlotte shook her head subtly and pillowed her wet face made by her tears of sorrow into her hands. She was still trying to battle disbelief and shock. Her best friend of 40 years sat beside her in a non-busy Apple Bees booth. Clara's right arm comforted Charlotte's shoulder as her head tilted to lean on Charlottes fiery red hair. "I'm so sorry baby, baby. I'm so sorry!" Clara told Charlotte. Their other friend Cady reached across the table to offer her support and comfort as well.

Charlottes husband Troy, of 25 years was not a runaway bandit. He was a prestige lawyer of Macon County Georgia that came from a lineage of wealth, power, and entitlement. He had served his wife divorce papers the same day he took all her finances away. He had paralyzed her financially and emotionally.

"You know I never liked that bastard." Clara (the feisty one) threw up her hands and spoke. "Clara!" Cady (the warm one) scolded. Clara's bottled-up anger begin to burst out. "It's true! I have never liked him since day one! Charlotte, He made you stay at home with the kids which kept you from finishing college. You put your personal life on hold while you took care of him in law school. You didn't get to pursue your dream career. All of your dreams and goals were dismissed. And you had to help build him up and what did you end up with? A sorry sack of shi…" "STOP!" Cady interrupted. Cady knew that her sailor friend was going deeper and deeper on a cussing binge, and her sacred ears would not be polluted by such foul talk. Cady and Clara gazed at each other as Cady nodded her head in reference to their

3

friend. Charlotte pulled her head up from her moist hands and began to wipe the clear snot running down her nose with the paper napkin that once held her silverware. "I'm so sorry yall." She voiced shaking and wiping her face. "Don't you dare apologize honey. You are not wrong for crying. You can breakdown all you want. We love you, Charlotte. We are here to help as much as we can." Cady chimed in.

"Yeah, baby baby. Why are you apologizing. It's ok not to be ok." Clara affirmed. "Now I did some investigation and come to find out that he's with that new little secretary. That little wench. And they have the nerve to buy a new dog!" Clara exclaimed. "Uggh Clara how is this helping Charlotte right now? And why did you spend all that money on a private investigator?" Cady questioned with a confused mind. Charlotte sat back in a daze as she listened to her friend's quarrel. She was physically there but her mental was occupied with regret and wonder.

"No honey. I am the investigator. No moneys were spent on this here endeavor." Clara stated. "Facebook is free to all. Baby all women know how to turn on their FBI, CSI agent on. We get what we need from Facebook honey. No need to hire anyone." Cady shook her head and allowed her bright blonde bob to follow. Cady said, "Absolutely not. I will not play on the devils' playground." Clara voiced her frustration, "Oh for Pete and Charlottes sake! You are a 2024 Baptist Cady not a 1924 crusader. I mean Christian's use social media! Steven Furtick is on there all the time. And the way that that guy preaches, honey I'm sure he still is going to heaven." Cady shook her head in disagreement and disapproval.

"Now anyway." Clara started. "What we can do is…" "Hey guys can I get you anymore to drink?" The thin tall male waiter asked. "We're good." Clara said expeditiously in efforts to shoe him away from her still crying friend and her master plan scheme speech that she was trying to let out. "Like I was saying," Clara kept her eye on the waiter as he walked away. She began to talk when she thought he was out of ears reach. "What we can do is get some hot dogs. Fill the middle up with some chocolate. Wait until the dog comes out the house. Then we will throw the dog the hot dogs, and boom! Checkmate" Clara exclaimed. "You mean animal cruelty, imprisonment, murder!" Cady exclaimed.

Charlotte let out a brief chuckle. She was always humored by Clara's radical ideas. "I'm serious." Clara said sternly while watching Cady's blue eyes grow bigger and bigger. "I know you are," Charlotte chuckled again. The relief of laughter began to ground her back to familiarity. "That's why I'm laughing. That was a good one. Thank you, friend." Charlotte took a deep inhale and let out some of the burdens that clung to her chest. The stability of their friendship was an anchor. Clara was her muscle. She helped her stay strong. She grabbed Cady's hand and said "Thank you again for the sunflowers. I Love them." She referenced the bouquet of sunflowers Cady brought over three days ago. Cady was her heart. Always so caring and nurturing. She was a physical reminder that she was loved. Because not only did Charlotte lose her sense of self, but she also started to lose her sense of self-worth.

Sure, they didn't have a perfect marriage. But there were no detrimental reasons that she and the love of her life since she was 19 years of age, why they would ever get a divorce. And what about their daughters. Brooke was only 11 years old. Meredith was in her last year of High School. How could he rip the family apart at such a crucial time in their daughters' lives? It didn't make any sense. And for that reason, Charlotte was not able to truly grasp reality. Her thoughts raced around her head like a Nascar driver. 'What can I do? What could've I have done better? Sure, I have gained some weight. I'm probably not the ideal image. But since when did our love become superficial. What happen to his morals and values? I mean, I cooked every day. I took the girls to school every day. I never missed a soccer game or volleyball practice. I made sure I cleaned the house twice a day. I washed and ironed his clothes. I gave him massages. I have given him and my children all of me to the point where I don't know who I am without them. Without him. Without this. I was a good wife. I was an even better mother. I was a good person.' Charlottes negative thoughts began to flow over into her body in the forms of tears. She sat back and began to weep again. Her friends were helpless onlookers that were not equipped to instantly fix their wounded friend.

\*\*\*

### Three Months Later

"Mommy why are you making us hot dogs with chocolate in the middle?" Charlottes youngest daughter Brooke starred at the weird sight. Charlotte smiled "Oh, honey this is kinda like, you know, when we umm go camping and have s'mores. That's like how this is, only its a hot dog." Charlotte tried to cover up her mysterious behavior by incorporating real life scenarios, "Oh cool!" her daughter said. "Where's the marshmallows?" Brooke asked with curiosity. "That's absolutely disgusting." Charlottes eldest daughter Meredith protested while washing off green seedless grapes in preparation for her school lunch. Charlotte laughed. Her daughter was right.
It was gross.

The last several months Charlotte became insanely obsessed with being the best FBI detective she could be. FaceBook Investigator. Kudos to her bestie Clara, for all the long hours she would sit on the phone with Charlotte. She allowed her to vent, cry, and cuss at any given time of the day. The women would track down all the crime her soon to be ex-husband would be indulging in. This morning before the world woke up, his mistress posted that she was happily expecting a new bundle of joy. More like a bundle of scandals. A bundle of disaster. A bundle of hate and jealousy eroded in Charlottes once carefree heart. The audacity of this imbecile. The sad part was that Charlotte literally trained her replacement at work and unbeknownst to her, in her love life. She gaged at the last conversation she had with his then Secretary Brittany. "It's like you are a younger prettier version of me." A phrase she said so innocently to Brittany. A phrase that she now swallowed with a broken tooth and broken heart. Brittany's youthful face and frame was now the image of Charlottes envy. A divorce without a reason was heartbreaking to go through. A divorce with a skinny, beautiful younger woman as the contributing factor added unnecessary insecurity.

"Come on guys so that we are not late." Meredith ordered them while dashing to the front door of their grandparents' house.

Charlotte had to make the humbling decision to move back in with her parents once her husband kicked her out of their 7-bedroom lakefront mansion. The prenup was in both of their names. The house was only in his. Charlotte looked at her youngest daughter and forced a smile. Being strong for herself was nearly impossible. Being strong in front for her girls was a necessity. "Did you brush your teeth?" Charlotte asked Brooke. "Yes mom" Brooke dragged. "Mouth Check." Brooke blew her minty fresh breath slightly in her mother's freckled face. "Arm check." Charlotte requested. "Oh, I forgot deodorant." They both smiled. Brooke ran out the kitchen and upstairs to the guest room where her and her sister had to now share. The girls went from having their own rooms and closets. Living a carefree life. To now having to transition to shared spaces. Uncertain of what the future held. Brooke missed her home with her dad. Brooke missed the stability there. Brooke missed her dad being her dad.

Charlotte grabbed her keys, coffee, and chocolate filled hot dogs and met her daughter Meredith in the car. "Mom." "Yes baby" Charlotte responded. "Why don't you care about yourself anymore? Is your self-esteem that low that you have just given up on you? I mean you don't even get dressed or brush your hair. You just get up and go?" Meredith looked at her mother's tangled hair and oversized dad shirt and sweatpants. Charlotte realized that she had the same outfit on the day before. "I, I, I," Charlotte was thrown off. She didn't realize her daughter was so attentive. Her daughter could see her mom's life was a disaster in the way that she carried herself. Brooke joined them and said so bubbly, "Ok let's go now the princess has arrived." "Oh Lord" Meredith rolled her eyes and spoke. That was a great distraction to take the attention away from being drilled by her 17-year-old drill 17-year-old drill sergeant.

Charlotte pulled out the driveway reaching for her coffee that had disappeared. "Where's my coffee?" Charlotte said confused. "Oh, mom stop the car." Charlotte instantly pressed the brakes as Meredith requested. Meredith got out the car and returned with her mom's pink Stanley cup in hand. "You left it on top of the car mom." Meredith handed her mother the coffee and revenge hot dogs. "Thank you." Charlotte said to her daughter out of embarrassment. Charlotte presumed to take her daughters to school. It was hard to keep herself together when the world around her was falling apart.

Charlotte pulled into Bluevile High School and trailed behind a few cars off to the side. That was her normal drop off spot due to the embarrassment her daughter had of her. "Mom pull up. It's ok, I'll get off at the front." Charlotte was shocked by her daughters change of mind. Or was it a change of heart. The once embarrassed teen was now extending her hand of acceptance towards her mother. Meredith was her fathers, Jewel. A daddy girl since birth. Charlotte knew her daughter was a daddy's girl before Meredith became obsessed with Dora the Explorer. Her father would always take her fishing and read books to her at night. He was so active in her life. He was such a great father. How did he lose his sense of loyalty and provision? How could he just so easily break his daughters' heart? How could he wake up one day and just not care?

Charlotte hesitantly pulled up to the front. "You sure?" She quizzed her teen. "Mom. Life sucks for you right now. Like really bad. But I just want you to know that you are a good person. You don't deserve this, any of it. I love you and I'm so sorry dads being such a jerk." Meredith leaned in to give her mother a genuine hug. Charlotte fought back the unexpected tears. "Thank you, baby. I love you." Simple letters with a grand meaning. Meredith ran out the car to beat the bell. While Charlotte replayed her daughters' sincere words over and over in her head. "You are a good person."

***

## Three Months Later

Charlotte sat across her mother in her parents living room smiling with joy and relief. "Well, you don't have anything to say?" Charlotte questioned. He mother picked up her coffee cup and took a sip. Even though it was late night, the thunderstorm outside called for warmed hot caffeine. The thunderstorm that was brewing on the inside of her home called for a strong glass of wine. "Go get some towels for me please and bring them to me." Charlottes mother Caroline asked. "Sure mom." Charlotte said as she got up to fulfill her mothers' requests. Charlotte was in a state of confusion mixed with relief. Charlotte's ex-husband, Troy, had just met her for dinner earlier and told her that he wanted his family back. This meant no more divorce. No more trying to figure out what the further held. No more isolated loneliness. No more struggle. It also meant a long journey of healing and validation. Why now? Why did he even leave in the first place? The damage couldn't be undone, but she was glad that her prayers were finally being heard.

Charlotte walked back towards the living room, with the towels in hand. Her heart beating fast from the exert of energy her body eluded and the overwhelming mixed emotions her heart burst out. "Momma!" The living room was empty. She quickly noticed the sliding glass door to the backyard was wide open. The thunderstorm was blowing tree leaves and rain inside. Charlotte screamed for her dad and ran to the door in panic hoping the worst had not happened. Did someone break in and steal her mother? This kind of tragedy only happens in the movies. Charlotte put her thoughts to rest when she ran outside and saw her mothers' distant figure.

Charlotte ran to her mother who was digging in the dirt. 'Oh no she has lost her rockers' Charlotte thought. Anxiety struck but did not cripple Charlotte. "Mom, what are you doing out here?" The wind twirled their hair to and fro while the vicious rain continued to pour down on them. Charlotte began to regret the fact that she didn't think about grabbing an umbrella. Her mom came to her covered in dirt filled pajamas with two pairs of Charlottes favorite wine glasses. They were full of mud and water. "Hold these for me." Caroline instructed nonchalantly. "Mom! We have to go in." Charlotte yelled sternly. The howling wind and thrusting rain made her voice harder to hear in her normal use of tone. "Just hold these glasses honey." Caroline persistently asked of Charlotte. Charlotte grabbed the two Italian wine glasses in efforts to please her mom in hopes that she would be satisfied. Once satisfied Charlotte thought they could finally go back in the house. Caroline's shriveled small hands coupled her daughters face and then she began to smile.

THE WOMEN WHO SETTLE

She has completely lost all ounces of her sanity. Charlotte was convinced. "You know when you were little, I use to show you things physically so you could understand here." Caroline placed her left hand over charlottes heart. Understanding began to sprinkle in Charlotte's soul. Her mom wasn't crazy. She was trying to show her a visual example of something she wanted her to grasp. But was this necessary. "Your life is like this weather baby girl. Ugly and dark. And the rain is a burden that feels too heavy to carry. It's cold and dreadful here in this place. And here you are in the eye of a storm. Hurt and confused." Her words made Charlotte think about the reality of her situation. Despite what she thought to be good news of her husband wanting her back, she still had the stench of public and private rejection. And not to mention the embarrassment of him cheating and getting another woman pregnant. Another wounding blow she had not recovered from. There was unnecessary damage that she pushed in the background. For these past months she only focused on wanting her husband back, that she didn't even allow herself to process what that truly meant. And how did she expect to cope with the seriousness of all the negative consequences of Troy's detrimental actions.

"Don't let them cups go baby and follow me." Caroline instructed. They walked into the house drenched, cold and dirty. Caroline reached down and grabbed the navy-blue towels that Charlotte had previously dropped on before Charlotte she ran outside. Charlotte thought she was running to a rescue mission to save her mom. Instead, her mother was already on a rescue mission in efforts to save her.

Charlotte walked over to the sink to pour the murky water out and clean the glasses. Her mother stopped her in her muddy tracks. "Don't. I said hold them and don't put them down." Caroline said while wiping the rain off her face. "Mom, I get it. I'm ready to get dry and take a bath." Charlotte tried to say respectfully but there was an undertone of annoyance that Caroline picked up from her daughter.

Caroline walked over to Charlotte holding up the other clean towel. "Those fancy wine glasses represent your past and present life with your husband. The outside looks beautiful, exquisite, nice house, nice cars, financially stable, really, it's the American dream. But the inside of each glass represents the truth, the scandals, lies, heartbreaks, ugly and dirty. Why would you want to drink out of a cup just because its fancy? Despite the beautiful appearance, the truth is that what you are really drinking is fifth. Filth in your past life with your husband. And filth that will continue. Have you really thought about what he has done to you? And the work he would need to do to win you back. Charlotte you are the prize. Who you are as a person? You are worth way more. But you continue to settle. You are just so ready to accept a man back instantly that has destroyed you. Why? Because of familiarity. Because you are ashamed to be divorced. He doesn't love you, Charlotte. And he's shown you that. He's only coming back because he thinks you are easy. Like Sunday mornings at your grandma's house. Easy to leave, Easy to deceive, just easy." Charlotte stood in silence. An ocean of shock pulled her under. "Now!" Her mother pushed the clean towel towards her. "This represents your future life by yourself. It's cheap but it's the only thing you need necessary to clean you up." Caroline put the towel on the counter and spoke. "You choose." And then her and her wisdom walked away.

What a sight it was. Charlotte drenched and dirty holding 2 glamorous wine glasses, both worth over $2,000 each. Both were useless as they were filled up with symbolism of regret, misery, adulatory, rejection, lies and pain. With a regretful heart and a clearer mind Charlotte finally put the glasses down and grabbed the towel. She stripped down to her underwear and felt freedom taking off the layers of disgust that clung desperately to her body. And then the levy inside of Charlotte broke. Denial evaporated and reality took over. All the agony she held in exploded. Charlotte screamed violently in the towel in efforts to mute her rage and pain. She couldn't help herself anymore. The truth was ugly. She began to think that it wasn't a good marriage to begin with. But she made do. She had always been a people pleaser. Masking her true feeling and opinions with agreements and silence. She had been settling for years. Just so she could uphold the image of a beautiful life. Everyone around her was happy even if she wasn't. The embarrassment of the truth was finally out. Her worst fear wasn't that her husband cheated. Her worst fear was the hidden truth being exposed. Now there was nowhere left to hide. Nothing left to do but accept it. The truth was her marriage had ended years ago. She had ended when it began. But she was so good at ignoring the truth. It was just so much easier to pretend that everything was ok. It was way more beneficial to continue the unspoken agreement they both made for their children.

But what is a 40-year-old overweight, unskilled woman supposed to do. Who will accept these damages goods covered in grays and disarrays? Charlotte shook her head in disbelief. Even though fear tried to navigate her back to her safe space. Her safe space was toxic. It was unhealthy for her. Her mom was right. Her life was dark, her purpose was cloudy, and she suffered the consequences of her husband's selfish heart being cold.

Charlotte sat up and took a deep breath out. She was drained from the tears she just cried so viciously. She opened the door to her parents' fridge and saw a half gallon of country sweet tea, 6 capris suns, orange juice and Mascotto. She chooses the latter. Charlotte opened the cabinets and by muscle memory grabbed her favorite wine glass to drink out of. And then she stopped. It was part of the 4-piece set of the two earlier glasses that were still sitting on the table full of dirt and mud. Charlotte looked back in the cabinet and glanced at her mother's coffee mug. It was chipped and ugly, but sturdy. Charlotte paused for a minute and then put her favorite wine glass back in the cabinet. She then grabbed her mother's coffee mug. She poured the wine in the coffee mug instead and began to take a drink.

***

# 2 THE PRODIGY

"Do you know how many men I had to sleep with just to keep a roof over our heads. And when the food stamps ran out, how do you think y'all ate honey? It sho wasn't from my good looks that made that belly full. And it definitely wasn't from taking care of Mrs. Hattie and Lady Rue, only making $9 an hour, that kept us!" My moms' questions trampled my ambitions and detained my dreams. The knot in my throat got tighter and tighter as the sea drops slow kissed my cheeks. We sat in her 2003 Honda Accord in front of Mrs. Hatties house. My mom worked as a personal caregiver for the elderly all my life. She would also do in and out sort of jobs like catering on the weekends or tend to her cleaning service she never got legalized. Momma was stuck in the occupations they forced upon us so we wouldn't have shares and unions. The caregivers. And God bless the Negroe caregivers in the south that made half of what they made in the north. Still in 2024, the only thing that Burlington, North Carolina had to offer me was fried gizzards, and pig feet.
And I just turned vegan.

"So don't you come to me talking bout no make believes career. This is real work I had to do. Do you even know what all I had to sacrifice to keep you and your brother and little sister together,

complete and whole? I sacrificed my own mind, my time, my dreams, my goals. Just to make sure y'all could have somewhat of a decent life. And here you got a full ride to Duke University to be a nurse and you telling me you want to play make believe in
California. Ain't no way as long as I have breath in these here lungs of mines I'ma let you just go ways over to the other side of the world to do what? Be an inspiring actress? Ummm Ummm Nope! Baby the world will swallow you, spit you out, and then swallow you again just for fun, until you don't exist no mo. You need to be focusing on something stable, and steady, not just lullaby dreams. Now hand me my purse and cmon before Mrs. Hattie gets fretty because I took so long. And reach back yonder and hand me my switch cause MeMe bringing her three lil ones over later. And Ima whoop they hiney if they run around in dis house like they did last time. And wipe your face. Crying don't change nothing but your skin texture."

Momma exited the car while I finished sweeping the rest of my feelings underneath the rug. I grabbed the switch from the back seat like momma told me to and got out the car. Even though I was outside, in open air, I felt as if I was caged in.

***

## Three Months Later

"You need to stand up for yourself sis and stop being a lil pushover." My best friend Antoinette said while plopping down on my blow out, air mattress bed. "Dang girl when yo momma gonna get you a real bed? You been sleeping on this since the fifth grade. Don't your back hurt?" She teased while laying her hypercritical body comfortably on my bed. Her closed eyes and folded hands prompted her to pretend like she was about to catch her some zzzzz's. I finished pulling my crop top over my head and pulled my poetic justice braids up into a ponytail.

"Shut up Ann!" She hated that name. She said it was a whites only name and swore me to never utter it. And when I did speak it, she knew I was serious. Really, I was just being petty. I guess petty and serious. "I ain't got no other option. Besides how am I gonna even make a living all the way in Cali with no money, no place to stay, just a dream and ambition?" I took a deep breathe out after letting the reality of the words I just spoke sink all the way in and marinated my decision making. "That's just it! You not like me Courtney." Antoinette protested as she rubbed her belly. She was 7 months pregnant with her second child. Antoinette had her first baby when we were in middle school. I remember finding out about Kai the first day of our 8th grade. She threw up in our Spanish class when Marcus Hummeins walked by smelling like he dove and back stroked in a pool of axe cologne. Antoinette threw all her reduced/free school lunch up on his new pair of 23s and he was pissed. She ran out of the classroom, and I bolted out with her. That was Antoinettes first and last day at school that year.

I took a deep breath in and held it there. I was caught in the crossfire between what I really wanted to do and what my momma expected me to do. To most people moving away was scary. But to me I was excited and hopeful. But that hope was chipped away at, every time I spoke to my mother. The person who should be my number one supporter condemned my dreams and made me feel guilty of even having them to begin with.

"Courtney momma said you gotta take us to the park because we can't go by ourselves, and we need to go now." My little sister Kaila demanded. "Girl you and your bald-headed friends can wait. This grown folk's business." Antoinette snapped while waddling herself up off my bed walking towards my sister and her two best friends. "Now shut the door before I make y'all take turns rubbing my feet." Kaila started to cry. Before she left our room, she chorused her usual "I'm telling mommy!" "Good!" Antoinette yelled back while slamming the door. "Kids get on my nerves." I laughed at her comment while I placed myself carefully on the bottom bunk of my little sisters and little brothers bunk bed set. We lived in a one-bedroom apartment. Momma gave us the room and she slept on the couch. I guess going to college wouldn't be so bad. At least I would finally get my own room.

*\*\**

## Three Months Later

One thing my momma knew how to do was throw a party. My graduation party at my MeMaws house was stacked. All my uncles who really wasn't my uncles were there. My aunties who were really my moms' best friends were fighting over who was my Godmomma. And all my real aunties were fighting over which one of them I got my smarts from. The fish was frying, Hotdogs and Hamburgers were grilling. The music was blasting, everybody was laughing and hugging me. Everyone was having a good ole time. Everyone but me.

I disappeared into my MeMaws room to get away and allow my thoughts to settle. I looked through her closet. This woman had clothes for days. Especially church suits and hats galore. I picked out my favorite suit. It was the color prune purple. I grabbed the hat to match and started acting out the made-up skits that would come to my mind when I was daydreaming in my school classes.

"Courtney," My MeMaws voice startled me. I was caught red handed. I froze like I use to when she would catch me getting a pickle out of her pickle jar when I was younger. "I'm sorry MeMaw ...I was just…umm..." "Shhh child." Memeaw scolded. "I know you play dress up and record yourself on that there internets acting like you is me." My eyes widened from fear and shock. More shock than fear cause since when did Memeaw get a TikTok? The question buzzed around in my head the way honeybees danced around daisies. "Your cousin Neveah showed it to me." Memeaw said. I forgot that she could read my mind. She also had eyes in the back of her head. I shook my head and we both let out a big laugh.

"Sit down baby." I took a seat on MeMaws quilted covered bed. "When you were 2 years old you use to play dress up and run around my house in my heels and pearls. You could just be getting out of the tub and all you wanted on was my heels and pearls. We would be on our way out the door to church and guess what you got on?" "Your heels and your pearls" I giggled as I chimed in. I did remember those days. That was the start of my glamor imagination and make believe. I wasn't scolded at MeMaws house the way I was at home. Memaw was truly my best friend and supporter. Her telling me stories of my childhood made me feel all warm and cozy on the inside.

"So, what's wrong baby cakes? You're smiling but you're not happy." Of course she could tell something was bothering me. There was no hiding from her. She knew me better than myself. I was her branch. She was my roots. "I guess" I uttered out finally. I took a deep sigh and said, "MeMaw, I don't want to go to college. I know that to everybody it looks all nice and proper. And if I go it means that I made it out. But I don't like school. I don't like learning and I definitely don't want to learn about the body. That kind of stuff is boring to me. I want to be an actress and a model. I want to see the world and I want the world to see me. I want to have fun doing what I love. Why is that so hard for everyone to understand!" Wheeew. I puffed out. I needed that release. I never really get to talk about my feelings because I always get shut down with "You're A child so stay in a child's place." But I feel like MeMaw cared about how I truly felt. She was my safe space.

"Let me tell you a story chile." MeMaw started off. I looked at her with curiosity and wonder. Her stories came from a lineage of southern fried truths and a heritage of heartbreak and hustle. "There was this girl, years ago. She had big, big, big dreams of being this painter, an artist she called herself. She was good at it too. She could paint you blindfolded. That's how good she was. She hated this small little country town. She wanted to move far away from here and follow her dreams to paint in the big city. So, when she graduated high school, she did just that. She got the notion that she was gonna live by the ocean and paint the sea, and the birds and them big ole palm trees. She was convinced she would sell her paintings and just live her life carefree. Welp this young lady got to Florida and before you know it, she became homeless and pregnant. Turns out artists didn't bring in consistent money to keep the bills afloat. She found herself married to a mass manipulator, a drug addict, that beat her and cheated. Sometimes he did all in the same night. And all the warnings her family and friends said turned out to be true. It was a humble journey to return back home. But she panhandled $150 to get back to North Caculacky and she never painted again. Your mother is living out of fear, because I failed her as a mother. I didn't support her dreams. I wanted her to work in the factory. A good and stable job. Stability and

Security was what I wanted for her. Instead of helping her find her way, I let her get lost in it. We call that tough love. The Bible tells us that we supposed to train up a child the way THEY should go. Not the way we want them to go for ourselves. Courtney, baby God has blessed you since you were a little child to have a sense of style and fashion." MeMaw got up and went into her closet. She took out her treasured hat box that everyone knew was off limits. She handed it to me. I'm not going to tell you to do what makes sense to me. I'm here to support you on your way, whichever way you want to go. Open it." She smiled and nudged me.

I was scared and stunned. I never knew my mom was an artist. That was pretty dope. What a sacred secret to hide for so long. It made more sense as to why mommy was so hard on me doing what she thought was safe and secure. She didn't want to see me repeat her same failures and get hurt.

I opened the hat box, and it was like a million gazillion dollars was in that box. "Oh no MeMaw! I can't take this. This is …wheeww…whoa…" I paced back and forth with my eyes stuck on the box. My hands flirting with my hips and head. I stopped pacing so I could get clarity. "How much is this!" I pointed to the hundreds of dollars in the box. How in the world did MeMaw get all this money? MeMaw laughed and her belly moved while she did. My eyes and mouth stayed open. "It's enough in there for a year's worth of rent in California or a car to get back and forth while you are in school. It's your choice. She tapped my leg while she got up and left me with a mind full of questions, and a box full of hope.

***

### Three Months Later

I waited anxiously. I paced back and forth with nerves floating throughout my body. My palms were grossly sweaty. I heard the door crack open. My moms face had a frown. She walked in nonchalantly. "Hi mom." I said with the biggest genuine smile. "I see you not in school, so this where we saying our goodbyes?" My mom said, she made eye contact with me with a permanent frown. I didn't let her negative vibes chip away at my joy.

"Well mom. I just want to say thank you. For all of your sacrifices that you made. And I believe the biggest one was you settling for stability and throwing your dreams of painting, drawing away in the ocean lost at the bottom of your sea of sorrow and shame. She looked at me shocked. How did I know? Who told me her secrets? And how dare I dig up something she fought so hard to burry. Her questions were loudly silent. "So, no I'm not going to school, because mommy, I don't want to be a nurse and I'm sorry. And no, I'm not going to Cali either mommy." The waves of confusion showed up in the wrinkles on my mothers' forehead. "I have a new dream. I have a new hope. My dream is to see your dream come back alive and thrive." I finally was able to release my tears, and so was my mom. "What are you talking about?" My mom questioned. "Well mom this empty building is ours." I cleared the air of confusion. "I leased this space for five years. It fully paid for. Thanks to MeMaw." I smiled with clarity as she gazed in shock and wonder. Now she was scanning through every detail of the building with more precision. I opened the door to the far back room. My mother walked in with awe and wonder.

The room had canvases, a variety of paints, acrylic paints, fabrics, it was like an art supply galore. "This part is your art studio. So, you can paint, draw, sketch, or whatever you want to do. And for the front room I'm going to turn into acting and modeling classes for young girls to come and practice. I'm going to write plays and continue to explore my creative mind. I enrolled into community classes to start beginner courses until I can really decide what I want to do with my career. And together we can both operate in our gifting."

My mom, for the first time I had seen her, was completely speechless. My mom fell to her knees and just cried and cried. I got down beside her. "When did you transform into a such phenomenal, selfless, woman." She said through a broken voice and a drenched face. "I am who I am because you were selfless. And you sacrificed your dreams mommy. I'm thankful for you and I will always be a beautiful reflection of you." Sometimes compromising doesn't always mean you have to give up all you want to do. There's beauty when you let go. And

19

benefits when you take the lead. But the best option for me, was somewhere in the middle and in between.

\*\*\*

.

# 3 THE ENABLER

We sat in his bedroom on his King size bed in quiet. The white plug-in fan dismembered the silence. A chuckle followed by short laughter coming from the left side of me would occasionally make its appearance. Here I was a 33-year-old whore. Playing 21-year-old rejected love games. I was not the kind of whore that received payment for sexual pleasure. But I was a person who sacrifices their self-respect for the sake of personal gain. This situation-ship was personal to me. Emotionally satisfying and disturbing to me.

The room smelled like a pack of ft black and milds mixed with the aroma of failures. Both mine and his. The two of us were unequally aligned like my priorities. His problems were all superficial. Things that tarnished his image. Like a broken-down Denali truck, he was upset about. Not because he didn't have an alternative means for transportation to work, and the women's houses he went there after. His frustration fueled from the fact he couldn't drive up and down Nelson Ave with his Lamborghini doors up, blasting his sound system, while children and foolish women looked with admiration, and the men complimented him with jealousy.

My problems were internal. Spiritually I was stunted. And emotionally I was starved. I sabotaged my logical thoughts of my true ideal boyfriend to be congruent with my current man child "we're just friends" non boyfriend, boyfriend. I had owned my own trucking business and had leveled up to be a successful young black woman since I was 21 years old. But over the past couple years, and two toxic relationships, I had lost everything. And had no more fight left in me to get it all back.

I guess there's a point in every woman's life where she bows out. She has been broken to the point that something breaks within her brain. Her logic dissipates. Lucky is the man that catches this woman at her breaking point. She would settle for a man wearing a Jerry curl or a toupee. As long as it was a piece of love, she settled there.

I was troubled because I couldn't buy Martin's love. I tried too though. I put him in a house, paid his rent, gave him money whenever he needed, his phone was in my name, I paid that bill too, I had brought him a car, and did anything he asked of me. I made sure I made a way for him, even if I didn't have one myself. I couldn't sex him, loving me into existence either. No matter how well I did what I did when I did it, and yes, I did it all very well, it still did not make him see my worth. Why do we women do that? Think that men hold the same values we do when it comes to sex. Giving our bodies as an offering. Only for it to be a temporary satisfaction. Leaving both parties desiring more. Repeating this vicious cycle each time with hopes that maybe this time, he would love my sex so much that he would in return love me. Sounds foolish to say. Even more foolish to believe. I was his castaway. Alone on an island called love and loyalty. And the only one there was me. It had been that way for two years. I tried everything to break free. And the results all ended the same. I always let him back into my heart. But truthfully, as much as I tried to, I never let him out of my heart to begin with.

Martin started off as a Facebook friend, turned employee, turned confidant, that now fulfilled the role of my Mandingo Chocolate lover boy. But he friend zoned me like I wasn't special. Like I was just another random chick on his hit list. And that ate me alive and left active war wounds unhealed and very much present. But I wasn't new to rejection. So, I guess I just dealt with what I was used to.

Sure, there were guys (lots) of them that saw my worth and wanted to lock me down. But I settled for great sex and bad treatment instead. I didn't settle because I was strung out on the sex. I guess he just felt like home to me. I was comfortable in chaos; I grew up in it. I had been to 14 different schools and 12 different households. Simply put my parents didn't want me. For whatever their reasons were. See, I had met my father at 15 years old and he was high off crack. What an introduction to the man you have longed to see, touch, hug, and know for what felt like an eternity. The fact that he was on crack didn't bother me. The fact that he lived two streets over and never came to see me after our first initial meeting did. It was like pouring vinegar on lashed skin. Meeting him made the pain and curiosity more intense, not soothing.

My mother was the absolute best mother you could ask for when my older sister and I were little. It was just us three. She was a poor single black mother barely making ends meet. But she was rich in heart and love. We would make rice crispy squares together, watch movies while eating colored popcorn. Waking up on Saturday to Bebe and CeCe Winans or Whitney Houston meant it was clean up time. That was my favorite time in life. And then life happened to my mom. And I found myself at my aunt's house. And then back with my mom and now my new stepdad. This back and forth with other people in their places, and then back to my mom and stepdad's house, continued even through my High School years. So, I guess the dysfunction broke something in my brain that said people will love you and leave you. They will cast you away and it's ok. And that some love was always better than no love, from the people you love the most.

I had made Martin the ruler of everything because to me he was just that, everything to me. He put his black and mild out and lit his blunt. He looked over at me and then put his fingers in my nose. "Hey monkey." I guess that was his was of flirting. My nickname to him was monkey. I don't know why, especially when he looked more like a monkey than I did. His playful behavior at times made me feel young again. We bonded over trauma. His mother was a crack addict too. I pitied him.

The business men, pilots, and government officials that were all stable and showered me with love and admiration I did not want. I didn't know that kind of love. Because I guess that was not my normal kind of love. I was more familiar with rejected pieces of love. And my subconscious consciously fell in line with my adolescent orders.

He turned over towards me and got on top of me. This was my favorite position with him. Physically and emotionally. I liked being under him. Beneath him. It was something about seeing him on top of me, overpowering, that brought me comfort. My willful submission had cost me greatly. I had lost my true sense of self by allowing him to lead me in every way. The look of demand and dominance in his eyes while biting his lips made me fall deeper and deeper into his trance.

Deeper than his Mandingo strokes. This here was beyond sex. He knew I was his and his only. Knowing that made our physical connection intensify to a spiritual one. Although spirituality was something he did not believe in. He thought we came from aliens. I came from a lineage of ministers and preachers. Spiritually I was battling from within. I had made Martin my idol. My actions proved that he was my god. And it showed in every area of my life. My soul was in a tug of war. I didn't know how to break free and save myself. As much as my friends and family tried to help, only I could save me. Because I was the one that enslaved me.

Here I was, a 34-year-old whore in love and lust with a 32-year-old pimp. The sad part was we were both broke and broken. He needed me financially. And I needed to feel needed. I was his enabler. And he was my addiction. Martin was home to me, a familiar sense of what I perceived love to be. And so, I settled there.

\*\*\*

**Three Months Later**

We pulled into Love's Travel Stop for fuel. Martin put the truck in park and looked over at me, he extended his hand and brushed it over my nose before opening the driver door to exit. I smiled so giddily like my daughter did inside New York City's Target. And if you knew the joy and excitement my daughter Arianna had whenever she went to Target, then you understood the explosion of joy I felt in my inward parts.

I grabbed the keys from the engine and stepped out into what felt like negative 10-degree weather. My eyes began to water as the glacier wind whirled the snow and my frontal wig about in the air. I ran into the trucker's door like I was trying to escape the most vicious opp. The brutal cold. A man in overalls holding a tin coffee mug held the door open for me. The last few steps I slid inside like a football player did in the in-zone. The immediate heat that warmed my body made me

24

feel like I actually did make a touchdown, and the reward was utterly satisfying.

Thanks to my spidey sense, the first person I locked eyes on was Martin. He was invading the candy section two isles over from the trucker's entrance. His tall thin frame was hugged by a too little thin bubble coat. 'He gonna get sick', I thought. He wasn't prepared to be out in this brutal cold weather. And I wasn't prepared for this journey.

*Hey mom. I love you be safe.* A text message from my daughter Sophia centered me. She was the oldest of my three and quite the responsible one. I grabbed some Dude Wipes and replied back. *Thank you, baby, I love you. Have a good night.* I was what seemed like a million miles away from my babies. I was all the way on the west coast. Being a mother trucker was hard. The longer I stayed in trucking, the bigger my goals were. The more time away I spent from my kids.

We met back at the F350, and I was met with "What up lil monkey?" My mind translated his Ebonics to: "Hey companion." "You finna get sick with that to lil coat on. Why don't you get a coat in the store?" I asked Martin. He twisted up his fingers while using his California accent, "I'm good cuz." I reached into my purse and tossed him the dude wipes. "Go wash your men parts they dirty." I turned up my nose and spoke. "Dang cuz, you just gonna put me on blast like that! My stuff don't stink weirdo." Martin said while reaching his hands in his underwear. "Oh... never mind. I'll be back." We both laughed as he jumped out the truck to take a wash-up.

This was our second trip out together. I just brought the hotshot 4 weeks prior. One day we were in my semi-truck, and he pointed to a pickup truck that had a trailer attached. He had told me he wanted to do hot shot. A week later no questions asked I flew to Texas with $17,000. I put $13,000 down on the F350 and $2500 down on a 40 ft flatbed trailer. If it was in my power, then there was absolutely nothing I wouldn't do for him. Seeing him happy made me happy. And maybe just maybe he would see my true worth and truly love me? Love bombing much.

I looked down and he had left his phone. He had given me the passcode a few days ago while we were at another fuel station because I sent him money on cash app for fuel. DON'T DO IT VICTORIA! My inner sweet angel warned. Yep, I think Ima do it. I battled back with her. No, you will not! The sweet angel argued. I thiiiiiiiiink I'm finna do it. My bad side started to say. STOP IT! STOP IT RIGHT NOW! My angel of logic was fighting with my act bad angel. I named the good angel Monica and Miss act bad I called Young Florida. Girl if you don't pick up that phone and see what he really be on! My heart pounded. Young Florida was right. Victoria you can't unsee the seen. Y'all vibing right now. Play it cool and keep it a buck. Don't be desperate. Now Monica was right. I took a deep breathe in. Man forget that! You got plenty of time and the passcode. Type it in! And just like that Young Florida won. I picked up his phone and went straight to his messages.

The first message was from a girl named Monica. The irony. I scrolled through their conversations and the butterflies inside of me erupted with full force. He was so sweet to her. And she was sweet on him. The dialogue between the two looked like they had been together before, and that she had moved away and they were rekindling a new flame. A couple of "I miss yous" had my heart thumping but when I read the L word that came from his number and he actually sent it, I was knocked off guard by that one. Oh, so he know how to tell people he love them huh? Cause yep, I never heard that! Time out coach. There's a flag on the play. Take di whet leave di what? Who in the world was this girl? But more importantly who was this man? Siri please play Tamia there's a stranger in my house, cause homeboy was just so nice and sweet to her. He asked her how her day was and all I get was called lil monkey, lil dummy or a weirdo. Wow. The icing on the cake was her saying she missed their sex and it was soooooo good. I gagged. I rolled my eyes so hard until they locked in place. This negro expressed he missed her sex too. Dang Victoria. Looking a little defeated. Your name ain't holding its weight baby girl. Myself told myself. -10 points subtracted to my already low self-esteem. I exited out of their little love chat when I saw the nude pics she sent him. And him expressing how he wanted to kiss both sets of her lips. Oh really? You get like that huh? Cause it's been 2 years, 11 days, going on the 7th hour that we have been "Just Friends" with all the benefits and you only kissed both sets of my lips twice. I thought.

The embarrassment of my new reality settled in. He really doesn't like you, Victoria. His actions and his words have shown you such. And don't keep making up excuses for him. Face it. You are in love with your idea of who you want him to be. This is not love. It's a massacre. And your heart keeps getting slaughtered. I opened up the

message between him and his brother. Not him sending a pic of a girl with a booty bigger, way bigger, than mines talking about that's his new boo. I checked the date. Only a day after we just had sex in the truck. But guess what Victoria. You can't fault him. Cause you know why? He told you two years ago from the jump that "Y'all was just friends!"

I continue to break my own heart by reading multiple link up texts between him and various women. Me wondering who these girls were. Wondering did he use protection. Probably not. That's why my PH balance stay off. And I'm not even going to get on the fifty inbox messages from hood chicks, classy ones, black ones, Spanish ones, on Facebook. They were on big daddy like white on rice. The random chicks for sex didn't bother me. I knew he did that. But that Monica conversation did me in. He had told her he loved her. Something he never said to me. But what really took me out was the conversation between him and his brother. He told him that I was dumb to think he would ever go with me and that he would have to be desperate to ever do so. Dang Vicky. That was the lowest blow.

I put his phone down and wiped my eyes. I called my girl Mercedes to vent to her. She said what all my friends would say in efforts to comfort me. "You deserve better Victoria and let that nigga go." I pulled myself together, crossed over to the drivers' side just in time before he came out.

"What up lil Monkey!" Martin said energized and happy. Act cool, act cool, act cool. I tried to tell myself. "Stop calling me that! You the one that really looks like an ugly monkey!! So, STOP!!" Welp I did not listen to myself once again. As hard as I tried to act like nothing happened. It just did. I was literally traumatized by the truth. "What's wrong with you lil bald head?" Martin questioned in efforts to understand what he already started to suspect. I rolled my eyes and said, "I'm just tired." I played it off well. "Well, why you in the driver seat dummy. I told you I'll drive the rest of the way." Martin expressed. I changed the car phone to my phone and put on Mariah The Scientist and Summer Walker playlists. "I got it" I lied. It was dark. I was tired.

I didn't have it. I didn't have it together. And I just realized that I didn't have him either.

***

## Three Months Later

"Can I stay awhile?" I pleaded. "No Monkey. I'm not leading you on no more." Martin stated. And there it was. The words that freed me but clipped my wings all at the same time. My reality smacked me with a fresh switch from my grandmother's yard. I was struggling just trying to keep my composure. This is it I thought. This is what I needed to hear, but didn't want to. No matter what I went through with Martin, my heart craved him. My soul craved him. My body craved him.

Don't Panic. My inner strength rehearsed over and over. Let's be logical Victoria. You need this, embrace this and just walk away. I tried to tone down my sniffles while holding my eyes wide so the tears and snot would not run out. And then, I looked up at him. And in unison they dispersed like a broken fire hydrant. He shook his head and got up from the couch complaining. "See." Martin said with clarity while pointing at me. "That's exactly why you can't stay. You can't try to be in a relationship with someone who is single minded." He shook his head and plopped back down on the couch. Meanwhile I was trying to refrain from having a meltdown and looking crazy. DO NOT DO THE UGLY CRY VICTORIA!! My inner warnings could not overpower my actual emotions, and there it came. The ugly cry rolled out alongside embarrassment. I couldn't help it. As bad as I fought to keep it all bottled in. Thoughts of never loving him. The scarce thought of letting him go. Thoughts of never being loved by him. All these thoughts just flipped a broken switch on that wouldn't cut off.

I left his house with a wounded soul and ego. I stopped at a red light and went through my voice messages so I could hear his voice. I

28

saw a message 2 weeks ago that I hadn't played yet. Hmm, I thought, I wonder why I didn't listen to this one. Probably because all of his voicemails were him accidentally not hanging up. There were only recordings of him talking to unknown voices. I hit play as the light turned green. "What's up lil monkey!! Do You know why I call you lil monkey?" WOW he actually left a message. I was shocked.

I pulled into the Speedway and parked my car to fully listen. I hit play to resume his message "When I was little my mom had brought me this little orange monkey for my 7th birthday. I loved that monkey. It was like my comfort. Give me that monkey and a Pepsi and I was good to go." He chuckled. I was intrigued at the direction of his confession. "That same year my moms went to jail. Everything changed for the bad. And all I had was that little monkey. I don't call you monkey because I think you are ugly. You are so beautiful to me. You are a good woman. I call you monkey because you bring me the same comfort that that toy monkey did. I wish I could be a better person for you because you deserve that. Any man would want you. I'm just trying to get my life together that's all. But I do love you. Anyways lil dude pick up the phone silly. I miss you." I gasped at each and every word that came out of his mouth. The words that I longed to hear for so long. Two lights ago I received the perfect amo to finally break free. And like always something draws me back in. I scrolled down to the Bs in my phone and hit the dial on the contact Big Daddy.

"What!" Martin yelled through the phone with annoyance. His aggravation didn't deter me. I was use to his anger. "I forgot to tell you that there was only one Pepsi left in the fridge." I said calmly. "Yeah, I know." His tone turned softer. "Did you want me to grab you some more before I left this side of town?" Of course, he did. I asked just so I could hear him speak. He took a hit of either his blunt or black a mild and blew it out over the phone. "Yeah, and grab me some more FT's. Ain't no food in here either dude." Martin said. "What do you want to eat?" I questioned. Knowing good and well he was gonna say he didn't really know. I had to think for him most of the time. "Hmmmm it don't matter for real. What you feel like?" Martin asked. "Passsta." I exclaimed. "Yeah yeah yeah get that lil chicken and shrimp joints." He was getting excited. "Ok I'll be back there in a few." I assured him. "Alright little monkey." Martin said and then hung up.

This time when he called me lil monkey my heart sunk. I knew the true meaning of why he used it. I was his comfort. I was his home. And the cycle of no matter how bad he tried to not need me, and no matter how much I tried to refrain myself from him, continued to repeat itself. We needed each other in the most self-sabotaging ways. This time I didn't use fingernail clippers to clip my wings. This time, I used razor blades.

***

# 4 THE HURT HEALER

*"Teach the slaves blind obedience to authority, as questioning any white person is deemed disprectfull."* I sat across my supervisor with these words spoken by Willie Lynch at the forefront of my brain. My DON had such a deceptive attitude that tried to hide her true agenda. To discredit and denounce me. But I knew a serpent at first glance. This was the beautiful struggle of being a black woman in the corporate world. I deemed it beautiful because what didn't physically kill me. Only made me stronger mentally.

"I'm not signing this." I shoved the paper back over to her side of the table. I was angered by all the stunts she tried to pull to get me fired. She had written me up twice in one day. To the higher ups I was considered the disobedient slave. The one that didn't play by their rules. I allowed my moral compass and nursing knowledge to guide me. And they hated me for that. The fact that my skin had natural built-in melanin was another reason I was pushed down. They were trying to make an example out of me. They wanted to shut me up and put fear in the hearts of any other defiant nurse that chose to stand up for truth and ethics *"Take the meanest and most restless[ black person] inject them with the poison of self -doubt, self-hatred, and inferiority and you have a docile and submissive [slave]"* Another quote from the "Making of A Slave" by Willie Lynch. I had yet become submissive. I didn't hold my tongue when it when it came to exposing wrongdoing. And the scandals that we had in this company were enough to shut us down for good.

31

You would think for the 12 years I had being a nurse that I would know how to politic with the oppressor. But it just wasn't in me to do such. I was a wild card. Really, I wasn't built to take orders from the higher ups that cared more about financial gain instead of the improvement of their patients. That also cared less about the safety and sanity of the ones that delivered the care.
My heart was in the business of nursing the human soul back to health. Honestly, I should have gone in the direction of social work or psychology. But nursing paid more, and for that reason I dug my heels and nails in nursing and never took them out.

"Ok well I will let Sarah know that you refuse to sign. And I will let you know the next steps. As for now, there's no suspension so you can go and continue to complete your shift." Lindsey said with a half grin. "You mean you don't have another nurse to run my 3 units, so you aren't walking me out now because God forbid you have to do a med pass on your own." I got up and walked out of Lindsey's office before I allowed her to respond. I was over it, over this, and completely over her. I already had a target on my back. I could feel her disgust glare me down as I walked out of her office. I walked into the too small bathroom with two miniature stalls a couple of feet down.

I was emotionally drained. Previously my best friend of the last 4 years and work bestie had just been fired for a made-up reason. The brutal game in nursing was that if the people in power didn't like who you were as a person, not as a nurse, but as a person, then their plot to get you out of their way went into full force. Adrienne spoke up for herself and the safety of our patients, and less than 24 hours later she was gone.

I wet my face and sprinkled water into my golden Afro curls. My hazel eyes had a reddened glisten behind them. BOOM! BOOM! BOOM! BOOM! The 4 bangs on the bathroom door didn't startle me. I was always on my guard at work. "Let me in! Let me in NOW!" A 13-year-old voice demanded. I knew who she was and what she was trying to do. She was trying to AWOL. I went to the door to try to speak to her and calm her down. "What's going on Shasta?" I asked. I was a behavioral nurse at Precious Jewels Children's Residential Facility. It was a place where troubled teens were sent to in order to

THE WOMEN WHO SETTLE

try to help them with their behaviors. Most of the kids here left the same way they came.

"They trying to jump me! And I won't go back there. I'm sick of them. Let me in please!" Shasta cried. This was her daily routine. I could hear the drama and chaos on the outside of the bathroom. Before I could respond I heard two men move the youth down to the quiet room that was to the left of me. I opened the bathroom door to see multiple adults who were trying to regulate this disrupted teen. In front of me was as an open window with 6 feet of glass knocked out of its frame. Shasta had thrown something to break the window to come inside the offices. Off in the distant I saw 3 other disorderly teens trying to come through the broken glass in attempts to get to their target, Shasta. There were multiple team leaders and behavioral techs outside with the other three teens placing them in restraints.

I walked into the nursing station and saw the same scene that I did on a constant basis. The mental health Tech, Shontaye, that was supposed to be doing work was on her phone watching the latest episode of power. Her work ethic was piss poor trash and it aggravated my soul. "I just can't do this anymore, If they don't want me here then I just quit!" My frantic coworker Taylor said. She came in the nursing station seconds behind me and derived my attention away from Ms. At work but refuses to work Shontaye. "What's wrong boo?" I asked her while restocking the first aid kits. Taylor sat down in a rolly chair and began to ferociously put her hair up in a ponytail. "They keep saying that I'm crossing boundaries with the guys in the Emerald Wing. All I'm trying to do is my job." I tuned her out after I heard her say her first sentence. We had been down this road too many times. Obviously, the advice I had given her did not resonate within her. I nodded here and there as my mind ventured somewhere else.

"Help me please!" I looked up to see one of the male BHTS Raheem holding his neck with both of his hands. Blood was oozing out. My adrenaline jumped in. I looked over at Taylor who was frozen. I rushed to help Raheem. "Call 911 Shontaye." I instantly started barking orders. Shontaye was panicking around looking for a phone that was already in her hand. I pulled Raheem into the nurses' station and locked the doors. Our shift leaders Mewanie and Kelsey came rushing in. They were phenomenal nurses who always knew what to do. I learned so much from them.

Taylor was still frozen in shock. "Whhhat..Whhhat whhhhat happened?" Taylor finally let out. Kelsey looked up while applying pressure to Raheem's wounds and said "Two of the girls from the Ruby Wing slit his throat. How far out is the ambulance?" She refocused herself and spoke. Welcome to the trenches I thought. Where trying to save lives means that you are putting your own life at risk. Welcome my friends, to the beautiful field of behavioral health nursing.

***

## Three Months Later

I pulled into the Bob Evan's parking lot to meet my friends for brunch. Of course, I was late. I was always late. But to my defense I had to fight my way through a million dinosaur toys and LOL dolls to even get to my front door. My cheeks were still wet from the 37 toddler kisses from my son. I never wiped off his sweet suga. I saw my friend Adrienne in her blue scrubs, thick long hair in a ponytail walking in. I was bum rushed with excitement and joy. I hadn't seen my friend in a while. I missed her.

I was greeted by a huge smile from a very red lip from my friend Tianna. She was a vibrant soul that made the room more vibrant. "Hey girl!" Tianna said as I sat next to my other friend Kelsey. Kelsey was a single mother of one. Here natural wrap was trimmed to perfection. My other friend Mewanie blew out her vape and said, "Trick you late." She was of Philippine and White descent, but you couldn't tell her she wasn't black. We all came from different backgrounds and cultures. Some of us believed in God, Mewanie believed in Buddha. Kelsey didn't believe in either. I loved the fact that even though we had our different beliefs, it didn't take away from our friendship. We believed in each other. And that was the foundation of our sisterhood.

"I'm sick of this nursing crap." Kelsey said drained. "I'm just over it." Adrienne chimed in. "It's like we fight so hard with hopes that we are really gonna make a difference in the lives of people. Only to get into a game that's already rigged. If you care and show that you care, you get faulted for your compassion. What sense does this make?" Tianna questioned. "Go to school they say. Become a nurse they say." I laughed and spoke. "Here I was thinking I would have a career that made enough money which would allow me to spend more time with my kids. But the 9-5 wages are laughable. So now I'm forced to work more hours and go back to school so that I can get paid more. Which means even more time away from my kids." I stressed. I was an LPN in school to become an RN. Being a single mother trying to pay all the bills, and balance being a mother was a burden for me.

"And what about the burnout we face." Kelsey chimed in. She was a highly decorated RN. "I'm still trying to recover from the trauma of being a Covid nurse during the pandemic. I mean seeing someone smiling and walking and then 10 minutes later, they code and die. I can't tell you how many people I have tried to save that passed away with me pressing on their chests. Mentally I think I need help. That's not normal." The reality of how challenging nursing was on every angle impacted us all. "Forget nursing let's just go rob a bank." Mewanie lighten us all up and said. We cracked up. Because there was truth in her suggestion to switch careers. "Man, I'm one bill and one call away from calling the dope man." Adrienne said. "My cousin lives by the ports in Florida." I winked and added.

"So, what do we do? Continue down a path that no longer suits us? Or change careers. But that's not feasible either. On the flip side who wants to live life unable to do what you truly love to do?" Tianna questioned. This was real for all of us. "Tianna baby, when you got bills and skills, what's love got to do with it?" Kelsey ended the conversation with the truth to bring our complaints to an end. Changing careers would be nice. But at 30 something years old, and 4 mouths to feed, the only thing I could change was this 20dollar bill in my left pocket.

"With everything that I have going on, y'all sometimes I just feel like ending my life." Tianna started to cry and spoke. Where is this coming from, I thought. She looked so vibrant and happy. How could her soul be troubled when she had so much going for herself? I was unaware and unprepared to hear this coming from her. "Girl don't talk like that. You will be ok. You just need to get that no-good nigga out your life cause he's draining you." Kelsey was blunt and to the point. "No Kelsey don't fault her for saying that cause life be real for some people. You don't know what all she got going on. She must be battling with something? Tati what's wrong boo why you feel like that?" Mewanie asked. "It's not just him," Tianna shook her head and said. "It's everything. I just feel so angry and lost sometimes y'all. I don't know if I'm coming or going. Things keep going left and I'm just tired. Like what am I really here living for? To pay bills and take care of everyone else. Well, who is gonna take time out to take care of me?" Tianna's voice raised. The passion in her voice gave me chills. The hurt in her heart broke mine. I was silent because I knew the battle she was fighting from within. I too had the same thoughts and feelings at times. I never told anyone because let's be honest.

Black women don't kill themselves. We allow others to do it for us.

"I get it." Adrienne said. "Life changes and sometimes we aren't equipped mentally, or financially to deal with what life throws at us. But baby girl you do have a purpose. And if it wasn't so grand, then the devil wouldn't be planting those seeds of destruction in your head. You gotta fight and see the truth of what you are going through. The devil only wants to take you out because he knows how big of a threat you are to his Kingdom. You do good for people. You literally save lives. This calling you have on your life is beyond nursing. Anytime you are doing good to build up others and God's kingdom the enemy will do what his purpose is. Be your enemy. He's gonna try his hardest to try to defeat you. Don't let the devil deceive you. Change your music. Guard what you allow to be deposited into you. And I second Kelsey, the man in your life is taking so much from you and out of you, he's probably the main contributor to you feeling like this. Baby them bills can take care of themselves this month. Break away and get your mental and emotional health together. You got 3 months before they come and repo that car." We all started to laugh at what Adrienne just said. I decided to chime in, "You can take time to take care you. And I need you to fight for you. Cause I need you not to just survive this but overcome it. You mean so much to me and to us. I can't imagine my world, this world without you."

The cape we put on as Super Woman never comes off. We put it on in the morning when we get out of the bed. Before we brush the stench out of our mouths. Making sure our kids are prepared to conquer whatever the day has in store from them. We keep it on at work. When we deal with supervisors that don't see or acknowledge our worth. We have it on when we try to fly above their behaviors and detain our feelings. We use the cape when we come home and cook and clean. To pay the bills. In the bathroom where we try to regain our strength and sanity. Only for our little ones to barge in looking for you to produce Band-Aids. We never take our capes off because life won't let us. We are underserved, overworked superheroes. We heal those with the love and light inside us even when we are broken and hurt ourselves.

\*\*\*

## Three Months Later

I gave him my violence and he accepted it. He dealt with me tenaciously. I loved that I could be unapologetically me and he indulged in every piece. I didn't have to be the superwoman around God. I took my cape off at his throne room and was able to leave it there with him. The war within me was a burden. And I cast them all to Him.

I looked out into the crowd of youth girls and young women. Here on this stage, it felt like home. I wasn't scared or nervous to speak to them. I finally answered my calling. They say if you would do your work for free then it isn't work to you. Being a motivational speaker, philanthropist, idea distributors was at the peak of my bucket list of careers. Turns out I was going in the right direction, just on the wrong path.

"They teach you to watch out for the snakes in your grass." I said into the crowd. I was finishing my speech at the Annual Women's Conference in Columbus, Ohio. "They are visibly harmful and known to be deadly. But what they haven't talked to you about are the caterpillars in your garden. The subtle people that come into your life that bring you no alarm. So, you allow them in to nurture them. You have it in your mind that they are harmless and will eventually turn into beautiful butterflies. And before you know it these caterpillars have eaten off of you so much that your garden is now in ruins. Bite by bite they eat off your leaves. They have used you to benefit solely for themselves. And now they have enough to grow wings and fly away. And so, they fly away from you. You sacrificed so much in hopes that this beautiful butterfly would stay. They have taken you for all you have. Only to leave you with a ruined garden and empty cocoons. Empty promises. I'm here to tell you to look out for the snakes in your grass, yes. But what you really need to be careful about, are the caterpillars in your garden."

I gave the crowd a wave and the standing ovation left me speechless. I gave the host the microphone and walked off the stage. Who knew that actually taking a chance on me would bring me this far. I left the bedside, corner side, all sides of nursing 3 months ago and started to do what came natural to me. It took great courage to just walk away from what I envisioned my life to be. Fear was my caterpillar. It crept in through mini experiences of failures. Those experiences planted seeds of doubt to where my once vibrant and beautiful garden had turned into a chamber of weeds and ruins.

Luckily, I had a great support system that spoke words of beauty back into me. Those beautiful words and actions brought life back into my garden of dreams and aspirations. "You did it!" My older sister MeMe screamed with the proudest smile on her face. I smiled so joyfully and gave her the tightest hug. "Because of you." I looked at her with eyes of sincerity. Meme had given me a place to stay when I was transitioning. She helped me with my kids and let me stay with her rent free until I could get back on my feet. She was my superwoman. And I loved her dearly.

"Anything for my baby." She gave me the sweetest kiss on the cheek as she said it. On our ride home I couldn't help but wonder who my message really impacted. I prayed over the seeds that I just planted in the lives of those young women and hoped that they would live their lives in full potential without being used by people. I prayed that when life began to throw daggers their way, that they would rise above it all and soar.

*"I freed a thousand slaves; I could have freed a thousand more if only they knew they were slaves,"* Passing through the corn fields of nothing but vast land my favorite quote from Harriet Tubman popped into my mind. I lived half my life living out the expectations of others. The other half of my life I lived in survival mode. A lot of times we get caught in the motions of just doing life, but not truly living it. It's like we are robots, or more like prisoners. I'm glad I broke my chains off. I'm glad I was able to finally use my cape to benefit me. I'm glad that I flew away. I'm glad that I broke free.

# 5 THE DRUNK

Kim fell off the couch and was awaken by her body making contact with the ground. She grabbed her head out of pain and stumbled up off the floor to walk into her kitchen. Her pale frail body had on a size 2 blue dress that she had worn the night before. Her eyes played peekaboo with the time on the stove. And then she took a longer steadier look. It read 10:53. This better be nighttime she thought. She went to the kitchen curtains above the window. She pulled them back and was greeted by bright sunbeams. Low and behold, it was daytime. "Fudge!!" Kim said in a panic as she hurried to get ready for work. This was the 2nd time this week Kim was late to work, and today was only Tuesday.

Kim taught at an inner-city school where there were more dropouts than graduates. Her first stop was the school cafeteria. She needed some type of water and bread to help sober her up. She grabbed her necessities and saw a new student sitting by herself looking around. Kim sat down in front of her. "Hey, I'm Mrs. Lewis but you can call me Lil Kim." The young girl laughed, and then covered her mouth to try to mask her smiles. "It's cool, what's your name? Where you from?" Kim asked. The young girls attitude changed. "Mam can you please get away from me. I don't need you cramping my style. It's bad enough that I'm new. Now nobody is really gonna want to sit with me because a is teacher here." The young girl said. "Ohh, I get it. Kim Said, "You think this little white lady is cramping your style, huh? Sweetheart I'm here to help." Kim leaned in and said "Never judge a book by its cover. The good ones look boring." Kim got up and was only allowed to take two steps before she was bombarded by 6 teenage

41

girls. All of them were talking at the same time and fast. The thought process of these girls to actually think Kim could listen to and respond to each of them at the same time. "Whoa whoa whoa.
Ladies. Hold on. How about y'all sit down with me and we will go through this one at a time." Kim sat back down at the table the new girl was at and the other girls followed. "Now before y'all start this is my new friend…" Kim put her left hand out to prompt the young lady to say her name "Alexis." The young girl said shyly. "Oooh that's a cute name." One of the girls said. "Yeah, and your hair is popping! Who is your home room teacher let's see if we in the same class." They turned all their attention away from Ms. Lewis and made the new girl feel comfortable. Kim got up in the midst of the new friendships that were being established and smiled. The new girl Alexis smiled and waved at her. She was wrong about Ms. Kim.

Kim walked out of the cafeteria and noticed one of her students with a hat on. "Kyree you know I cannot pass you and allow you to keep that on kid." Kim said regretfully. "Ms. Lewis, you don't understand. My moms wanted to save money I guess; I don't know what's up with ma dukes but she cut my hair bro and this ain't it?" Kyree said shamefully as he took half of his hat off to show Ms. Lewis. "Oooh I see." He had multiple bald spots on his head. It looked more like a mockery. "Ok listen, go to the office and get a pass so no one else stops you. I'm sure principal Steven's will allow you to keep your hat on for today." Kim said. "No Principal Steven's wont. The rule is there are no hats to be worn in the building. So, there will be no hats. No exceptions. As for you Ms. Lewis you can join Kyree at the office, please." Principle Steven's said sternly to both of them. She's such a wicked person. Kim thought as she followed Kylee to the office.

"Kim, I have been trying to be patient with you. But I can't let your work ethics continue to disrupt the stability and educational growth of these kids." Principle Steven's was a prominent African American woman that had a background in law. Her medium sized dreads hung long enough to touch her African inspired suit blazer.

Kim had been teaching at St John's High School for the last 7 years. She was a stellar teacher. She taught in a way that the children could relate to. Despite how phenomenal she was as a teacher; her personal failures overshadowed her strengths. She would have great days normally. But her bad days were the worst days out of all the teachers. For whatever her reasons there were times when Kim drank and still was functional-able. But there were times when Kim let the alcohol take over. And the disfunction in her life overflowed into her work. "You only have two options. Either You take a breathing test, and it goes on your record. Or you must go to rehab, right now. There will be no consequences if you choose to go to rehab. And you will still be paid your salary. You need help Kim. And I don't want to lose you to the bottle." Principal Steven's gave Kim her final options.

"No way, I'm not doing rehab. I'll blow." Kim said thoughtlessly. The stigma attached to rehab made it even harder to get Kim to go there. In her mind Kim didn't have a problem. She grew up with an alcoholic for a mother. She didn't sell her body for booze. She didn't take the rent money and bet it all on black just to come back home sober and broke. That was her mom's gig. Not Kim's. She was better than that and she didn't need rehab. "Kim, if you blow even a point of alcohol than I will have to call the cops. They will arrest you for being intoxicated on school grounds." Mrs. Steven's pulled out her last card. She knew Kim would be a hard cookie to crumble, but she was determined to give her the help she needed.

"How long do I have to be there." Kim said with less confidence. She remembered she took a little swig of liquor before she got out of her car. She did it so she wouldn't get too sick. That little swig was for sure was still in her system. "Three weeks only. That's all you have to do. And then you can return back to school." Mrs. Steven's said. Kim looked at her with hate and demise. Who did she think she was putting Kim's back against a brick wall. Kim replied, "So are you taking me or do I gotta call an Uber."

***

## Three Days Later

"Now grief has various stages, does anyone want to tell the group where they are at in their grieving process." The group leader Michelle said to a group of 7 men and women that were all seated in a circle. This particular group was for beginners. People that just arrived at the Greater Love detox center in Virginia within the last week. There was too talkative Johnny who was from Oregon. He was a lonely man that only kept the company of Vodka. Jose came all the way from California. He was a drunk as well that couldn't function without Mary Jane. Micah was a beautiful blonde Instagram model that sold her soul to men on Snapchat and Pornhub. She was addicted to fentanyl. Shalom was everybody's brother from another mother. His peaceful tone and stature made a lasting impact on everyone's life. He was battling his demons of Suboxone. Cary was going through a divorce and Mr. Jack Daniel's was her new husband. Paul liked acid. And he was barely making it.

Everyone chimed into the discussion. Everyone but stubborn Kim. "I'm not grieving." Kim said with fury. Her posture was an outwardly expression of the resentment she carried on the insides. Her hands folded and knees were crossed. She was an introvert that refused to allow anyone inside her brutally cold heart. "Well surely there's an unspoken reason why you are here." the group leader Michelle stated. "There's got to be a reason why you drink.?" All eyes were on Kim. She hated the attention. "Because I'm thirsty." Kim said and then walked out through the side door.

Kim was over the small groups, big groups, alcoholic groups, just all groups. She lit a cigarette and took a deep puff in. Oooh this is what she needed. Nicotine. Crazy this place would let them have vapes and cigarettes but no caffeine. Kim looked over to the only seat that had shade. It was a swing covered by a gazebo. Kim walked towards the swing and took a seat. She started to listen to the bird's chirp. They probably were fighting over worms. Her destructive thoughts stunted her growth.

"Can I sit here?" A bright-eyed teenage girl said. She was covered in tattoos and bullet wounds. Kim was about to say no until she saw her belly. "Well, I'm smoking." Kim said dryly. "As long as it's not crack, we're good."

Normani smiled awkwardly as she positioned herself to sit on the left side of Kim. "I'm Normani by the way. I been here for about 3 weeks now. What bout you?" "Lil Kim. I don't know why I'm here honestly. But I guess I'm here." Kim said miserably "What's your poison?" Kim Asked Normani

"Welp I'm addicted to crack and fenny. And as you can see, I'm pregnant. So, I came here to get off that stuff man. I'm done with it for real this time." Normani shamefully said. "How many kids do you have?" Kim questioned. "This will be my 3rd child." Normani said while rubbing her belly. "Geesh, you look to young to have 3 babies." Kim stressed. "Yeah, I'm 17. I had my first child at 14 years old. One day I'm playing with dolls at my best friend's house. And the next day her stepdad tells me I'm beautiful. A couple days later I pledge my love and loyalty to him. I allowed him to do whatever he wanted, whenever he wanted to me. Once I started showing, he told me we was gonna run off and be in love together. So I left with him. I had the baby in the bathroom of a motel. He took the baby once I gave birth and I never saw it again. I don't even know if it was a girl or boy. After that I had to make sure we had a place to live. So I did what I had to do to make sure daddy was happy. And to make sure we had food and stuff." Normani told the tragedies of her life with closed emotions. "Let me get this right. Your best friend's stepfather, raped you, abducted you, and pimped you out?" Kim bluntness put Normani on the defense. "Naw it ain't like that. I mean yeah, kinda like that but he loved me. In his own way. I mean I know now that what he did was wrong. But its different when you are living in it. Honestly, he did love me but the world said it was wrong. And I love him still. It was torture to have to put him in jail and stuff cause for so long he was all I knew. I woke up in the hospital with 5 bullets in my body. I don't remember what happened. I can't bring myself to believe that he tried to murder me. But I did it because it wasn't all the way right for me to live like that. My mom said in order to get my second child back I had to press charges. But after all of that, I'm still alive. Thank God." Normani let out her hidden secrets and began to un layer her traumas.

Kim was frustrated at her ignorance. "How can you thank a God that allowed you to go through all of that. I mean you were shot five times!" Kim exclaimed with anger. Normani looked at the bullet holes in her wrist. "Shoot, I'm still alive, how could I not."

***

### Three Weeks Later

"Welcome back Ms. Lewis its good to see you on time and dressed so nicely. I didn't know that you had such beautiful blonde hair." Principal Stephens looked at Kim Lewis who had her hair pulled up. It was shocking to see that she was actually wearing business attire for the first time in years. "Yeah, it turns out, that dirty blonde was just dirt." Kim said with laughter. Kim was refreshed and rejuvenated. It had been almost 4 weeks since she last used alcohol to numb her hidden pain. Towards the end of her stay at rehab she had began to open up more about her addiction, and her reasons why. She had a sponsor now and continued to go to meetings. She found a counselor that she could relate to as well and was on her path to healing.

"Before you go to class, I need to speak to you about something." Mrs. Stephen's said while answering her phone. Kim stayed in the office for a few minutes and then mouthed "I'll come back" to give the principal privacy. Kim entered her classroom and began to get hugs from all her students. They had missed her so much and she missed them. Kim was happy to be back teaching again and started to take attendance "Kaya" "Present." A familiar voice said. "Kyree…Kyree?" the room grew still as Kim repeated his name. The students looked around at each other. "Where is Kyree he's never late?" Kim stated. Finally, one of Kyrees friends Andre said, "They ain't tell you Ms.

Kim?" Kim scratched her head in confusion. "Tell me what?" "They found Kyree in the attic. They said his mom and stepdads was doing some wicked stuff to him. Killed him." Kim's chest grew tightened. She tugged at the clothing near her heart. She for sure was having a heart attack. She tried to catch her breath, but it was all to heavy. She made her way back to her seat and begin to massage her head that was pounding. What in this sick world? Was the jacked-up hair cut a sign of abuse? Was I too drunk to piece it altogether? I could have saved him. I could have helped. And what about the time he asked to spend the night at my house, but I said no. Why didn't I ask him why? Or were my plans to go to the bar more important than finding out his reasons?

Kim's tornado of questions tore her insides up. For the entire 45 minutes left in class they all sat in silence. The kids were relieved when the bell rang. They all bolted out the door in awkwardness. Kim sat in her chair unhinged by the events going in and out of her classroom. She never heard Principal Steven's come in.

"Ms. Lewis, I meant to be the person to tell you." Principle Stevens said calmly while standing in front of Kim. "Did you know that I use to be a real estate agent before I became a teacher?" Kim looked up at Principal Steven's and said. "I was good one too, really really good. My husband and I had a beautiful 5-bedroom house in the outskirts of town. Everything was built from the ground up. And my son, can you believe that he wanted to be a teacher. He got accepted to 5 Ivy League schools to become a lawyer. But he said he felt called to teach. To make a difference in the world. I couldn't believe it, my son making pennies as a teacher. His junior year he had joined this church, and they were so active with the youth. Next thing I knew it was everything about God. God this and God that. Mommy God God God. He told me God called him to teach that's why he wasn't going to Law school. Can you believe the craziness? He loved God much. So, I don't understand, why God didn't love him back." Kim began to cry as overwhelming sorrow fused out of her while she was exposing her feelings. "He didn't even get a chance to live his life. On his graduation night me and him get in this stupid argument. And I tell him He's going to go to Law school. I was firm. No other choice. And he's battling me and his dad. And it's pouring rain. The kid barely knew how to drive because we drove him everywhere. But he takes my keys and dashes out the door. All the while I'm screaming in this pouring rain. Chasing after him because this stubborn boy didn't know that my brakes had went out earlier. And foolish me I was in a rush, and I should've just gotten it towed to the mechanic shop. But I put it off until after his graduation. And He can't hear me because of the downpour of the rain. And I'm pounding on the window, screaming 'The breakers don't work the brakes don't work!' And he's got the music blasting tuning me out because I have cursed his God and he's mad. He starts the car and pulls off."

Kim paused to let her tears bring salvation to her table. "Not even an hour later the sheriffs are at our door. How does one digest that their anger or their negligence or the combination of it both, were the reasons why your baby boy has died. There is no comfort for that. Did I want to lose my son? Did I want to lose my husband and our house? No. Did I want to end up a drunk? No. Did I want to teach kids, this is his dream. And the only way I can feel close to my baby who is 6 feet under the ground, covered with dirt, was to do what he said he loved. And maybe he could forgive me."

Principal Steven's wiped the tears from her eyes and held Ms. Lewis Hand. "You think that my drinking is the problem in this world? Take a look around. Go three blocks down from here and you will see a mother who has twisted thoughts in her brain to kill her own son. And then she stuffs him, in the attic, like he's not human. Go two more streets over. And you will see the problem for Kalesia is that

48

she's living with her rapist. And that's just too much trauma to think about. So, she doesn't think. Her brain switches off because it's been broken beyond repair. So, this precious baby girl can't focus in school anymore. And let's just forget about her graduating. Because before she's 14 she's in the hospital pushing out her stepdad's baby. And poor Tony who's been bullied all his life because his momma is too poor to buy him new school clothes and shoes. But the dopeman isn't. So, he manipulates him into thinking that a handout comes with loyalty. And he gives him money too. Now Tony decides he likes the power and influence of having a couple of dollars in his pockets. And the brotherhood of a gang. So, he starts to sell everything on the corner. And stops coming to school. And if he's not in jail for shooting the gun, he's the one in the morgue that just got hit by one. That's Problems! The real problem is that I started out with 27 students and now, I only have 9 that are graduating this year. NINE!!! This white lady drinking to keep her sanity is not the bigger of our problems." Kim said as she stared at Principal Steven's. Eye to eye, soul to soul.

There was a shifting in the atmosphere. Now Principal Steven' didn't see Kim as just a worthless drunk wasting her potential. She saw a mother that had experienced unexpected unmeasurable loss. She had bad days and worse days. On her bad days she could cope without a vice. On her worse days she needed help. "Do you want to go get a drink?" Principal Steven's asked Kim. Kim looked at Mrs. Steven's and pulled open the bottom drawer to her desk. She took out a half bottle of Jack Daniel's and poured Mrs. Steven's a shot. Mrs. Steven's raised her glass to Kim while she poured the liquor into her mouth. Kim took a shot out of the bottle. Today was one of those worst days for the both of them.

# 6 THE TRADITIONAL MOTHER

Bilan woke up to the sound of Chickens conversing to the heavens. She nudged her little sister Fawzia to get up and get ready for morning chores. "I'm too sleepy sissy" her 9-year-old sister was lazier and more spoiled than she had ever been. "Papa will feed you to the chickens if you lay here another minute." Bilan scolded. "Come, we must go fetch water to wash." The girls got up together and grabbed the families buckets to start washing.

Outside their mother had their baby brother on her back. And another little brother in front of her. Their eldest brother was already off to school. "Hello my beauties." The girls' mother Aamina said. "Who are you?" Aamina quizzed her daughters. "I am the descendants of Aamina and Bishaaro Ahmed. We are children of royal blood. I am strong like the lioness and wise like the eagle. I am a fearless warrior within. I bring beauty and blessings." Bilan and Fawzia both recited their morning affirmations to their mother. "That's right." Aamina smiled at her daughters. Their journey into the city was a tough one but necessary.

They arrived in town and went to a Women's Health Clinic ran by the Americans. Aamina told her daughter Bilan and Fawzia to watch their brothers Dalmar and Cubar outside, because there was no extra room in the clinic for them. "Aamina Ahmed?" The missionary nurse Zoe called into a hallway full of Somalian Muslim Women. Even if they were regular clients, she wouldn't have been able to identify them due to them being covered fully with the Niqab. However, the eyes were truly the windows of their souls. And when Zoe looked into Aamina's, she could see that something was troubling her.

Zoe smiled at Aamina while she motioned her to have a seat. The translator came in and Zoe began her examination. "Hello, I am the nurse practitioner for today and I am going to start with your vitals. Do you have any issues or concerns that you would like me to address?" Zoe said while checking Aaminas' blood pressure. Aamina was resistant to speaking but she couldn't control her pain anymore. She felt that her hidden trauma was free to be released. "It's so so painful, down there. Something is wrong." Zoe understood the cultural practices specifically the ones that the women of Somalia partook in. She had a pre-notion that the painful complications that Aamina was experiencing was due to female genital mutilation.

"Does it hurt when you urinate? Are your menstrual cycles painful?" The nurse practitioner asked. Aamina was ashamed of the truth. Yes, to all of the above and then some. Aamina thought. Aamina shook her head yes and looked away. Zoe gave Aamina some privacy so she could get prepared for her examination.

Upon completion of examining Aamina, Zoe found severe scar tissue and an open infected keloid along the sewn-up part of Aaminas vagina. Aamina had gone through the most harmful form of female genital mutilation called pharaonic circumcision. She went through this ritual at the tender age of 7 years old.

After giving Aamina medication and care to help alleviate the pain and complications, Zoe began to educate Aamina about the complications and dangers of infibulation. "Your daughters are at great risk. They don't have to endure the trauma and pain of getting cut on by a dull, rusted blade. Mrs. Aamina you know firsthand the excruciating pain that one has to endure for the rest of your life. This is your body, and you didn't have a choice, but you have a choice for the safety and health of your daughters. There are people in this world, a lot of people, who believe this is wrong. They have even passed a law banning female genitalia mutilation in this country. I know it's not the normal thing to do, but you can say no." Zoe continued to let her passion overflow as she pleaded with Aamina to reconsider the female circumcision of her daughters.

"Say no and then do what? Get beheaded in front of my daughters?" Aamina was hysterical. "What voice do you think I would use to say this. Because my voice is submitted to my husband. My body, my thoughts, my whole being is his. Even if it's not what I want. It's what I must do. This new talk I will not allow to ruin my traditions. My daughters' passage to woman hood is by doing this act. You can keep your western traditions. I'll keep mine."

Aamina became defensive because she knew there was no other way out. Who did this privileged colonizer think she was? Giving her options as if she had the actual freedom to choose. Aamina stormed out of the clinic in a hurry. Why would this lady bring this up? And now why did it burden her so much?

***

**Three Months Later**

Aamina woke up early for Fajr prayer. She started cooking liver and Sabaayad for breakfast afterwards. Today was the day her oldest daughter Bilan would pass into womanhood. Her mother-in-law traveled to stay with them for a month in preparation and after help care for Bilan infibulation.

Aamina began to think about the time she became a woman. How she went from a joyful playful young girl, to a wounded women for life with just one slice of a blade. After the painful passage to womanhood, she had to endure more pain every time she was cut open for childbirth and then sown back up. Maybe the woman from the Americas was right. Her precious baby girl couldn't handle this type of pain. What can I do to help? I would just be an outcast if I speak up. I will bring disgrace upon my family and husband for speaking out and against this. My thoughts do not matter, neither does my voice. Aamina thought.

"We are ready." Aaminas' mother-in-law looked at her and said, "Bring the child." Aamina pulled the strength from within to obey the orders she had been tasked with. It felt like she was leading her daughter down to the slaughter. Aamina had to be strong for herself and stronger for her daughter. Bilan was smart. She would be able to sense the fear in her mother's body.

Aamina tensely picked up her daughter and hugged her tightly. Before they left out the entry way Aamina said, "Precious, who are you?" "I am the descendants of Aamina and Bishaaro Ahmed." Bilan began to recite. "We are children of royal blood. I am strong like the lioness, wise like the eagle. I am a fearless warrior within. I bring beauty and blessings." Tears built up in Aaminas eyes. Her innocent daughter started smiling with joy. Joy that will soon vanish away. A deep betrayal she will never forgive herself for.

Aamina looked her daughter in her eyes and did the only thing possibly she could do to help. "Bite this. It will help." Aamina gave her daughter a piece of bitter root. Her daughter sucked the root and tried not to gag. "Eww mommy." Bilan said as she used her fingers to wipe her mouth. "Look at me Bilan. Remember you are Bilan. First born daughter of Bishaaro and Aamina Ahmed. You are stronger than the lioness and braver than 10,000 warriors." Aamina knew that this physical circumcision required mental strength. As she sent her daughter on her way to be cut, burned, and pricked on she wished she had the choice to choose. She would never choose this custom of humiliation and tragedy for herself and her daughters. Why did it choose them?

Aamina went to her room and pulled out her jewelry box. She intertwined the plastic pearls her daughters always played in in her hands. She held Bilans' favorite pearl necklace close to her heart, and then she began to cry.

\*\*\*

## Three Months Later

"So, if you see a child that is leaving overseas for a long time. Or
has a trip out of the country. Maybe they didn't let you know, and you
notice this child has had a long absence. It probably means that this girl
has went through or is going to be going through female infibulation.
Which is female genital mutilation. If your girl spends longer times in the
bathroom or has discomfort when they sit down, they probably have
gone through this horrific procedure as well." Zoe was educating nurses
and teachers at a Women's Conference about what to look for in the
Somalian Community to bring awareness and resources to Somalian girls
that were in America that still go through female genital mutilation.
"Being that 98 % of the Somalian population are still being circumcised
despite the global ban, we still have a lot of work to do to fight for their
rights and safety of these girls and women. Before it happens, we can
caution the parents and educate them on the many dangers female genital
mutilation imposes. After it's been done, we can still provide care and
resources.

Now FGM is grouped into four main types. Type 1: is where part
or total removal of the clitoris or clitoral hood is cut off. Type 2: is where
part of all of the clitoris and labia minor is cut, burned or/and removed.
Type 3 is where there is narrowing of the vaginal opening by sewing all
the labia and clitoris together. And type 4 is all other harmful procedures
to the female genitalia for non-medical purposes.

The safety of these girls depends on us. They have rights and is
FGM is considered abuse. Girls that are force to undergo such cruelty
have psychological trauma amongst the constant physical pain. Our goal
is to help stop it or ease some of the pain if it has already been done. We
provided

resources to aide in care such as pillows for the hard chairs for the school
agers. We host seminars and trainings such as this to help provide

awareness and resources about FGM. I'll be sitting outside the doors at my booth called M.A.D.I.S. Foundation which stands for Making A Difference In Society, because together we can, and we will bring about change. Thank you for your time." Zoe waved as she stepped down from the podium with the echo of hand claps and whistles that trailed behind her.

After her missionary assignment was complete, she returned back home to Cleveland Ohio to share her experience. She wanted impact her community and bring about change. Zoe sat underneath her daughters' nonprofit tent and asked her partner and Aunt, "Auntie?" "Yes" Her aunt Deborah said with a vibrant smile. "You know the song Pearls by Sade? There is a woman in Somalia…" Zoe began to sing. Deborah laughed and said "Yes, Child you know I do. And I see where you are going with this but continue on." "What if the pearls she was referring to wasn't just the rice, maybe the rice signified their own personal pearls that were stolen from them," Zoe said with heavy sadness. "And living life of tradition is a life you were born into but not one you would ever choose." Zoe continued. "And for that reason, child," Deborah said, "It hurts, like brand new shoes."

# ACKNOWLEDGMENTS

I have to thank God for giving me the beautiful gift of writing. It is my hopes that everyone that reads this book will be impacted, inspired and blessed by my works. Thank you to all the phenomenal women in my life that have given me golden nuggets to carry. To my mother Sharon Sullivan thank you for your beautiful gift of creativity. I am an extended branch of you. Thank you to my dearest friend Adrienne who has been my number 1 motivator, that celebrates my gift every chance you get. To the strong beautiful friend of mine Candice, you inspired me with this book idea and I pray you will find yourself in a place where you never look to settle. To my number 1 supporter, my friend, my sister, my cousin Latrice Curry thank you for all you have done to impact my life in a brighter way. To my dearest MeMe, thank you for loving me. I love and miss you. And to my therapist Mr. Traquan I am grateful for the self-love talks that you poured into me when I needed it the most. I love you all.

## ABOUT THE AUTHOR

Zoi Victoria is a Southern Belle with roots connected to North Carolina and Florida. She now resides in Columbus Ohio as a mother to three beautiful children. Her passion for writing started at a young age. She found an outlet through poetry and has won many awards for her poems. Zoi is a philanthropist, nurse, entrepreneur, and educator. You can learn more about her at www.zoivictoria.com

Made in United States
Orlando, FL
27 July 2024

49612305R00040